Fishing in Time

That is right.
Was it the code in your old notebook?
Right again.
Look out!
Wow! It works. Why not go time traveling?
The time slide is too small for me. But it did suck my notebook in!
Grandpa casts off again!
I have to get that book back or I can never fix the time slide!

The line breaks.
SNAP!
I will go get nore fishing line and a bigger hook.
Okay, Grandpa.
Do *not* send the line down again, kids. It is not safe for you.
t is time for action!
There is n answer here somewhere.
Yes! We go get that notebook! We can fit!
I do not know, Jill. I have not studied this yet.
What you need to study is *in* the notebook!
Okay. Just let me leave Grandpa a note.

Sliding through time!
YEE-HAAAA!

Now children are falling from the sky!
Ouch!

You must be the ones who stole my queen's crown!
It is bad magic, I say!
This is not good, Jill.

WHOOSH!
I guess Grandpa got more line.
GET THEM!
Look, Jill! The notebook!
WHOOSH!
Now, Will!

That must be your book of bad magic!
Will—look out!
Yikes!
This way! Jump!

Grandpa has sent a BIG hook for the kids!
Hurry!
This is it! Jump, Will!
Back up the time slide!

That was close!
That was great!
What did I tell you kids about that time slide?!
You said not to send the fishing line down!
And now that you have the notebook back, this will not happen again. Right, Jill?
You bet!

THE WILD WEST

Ouch!
PLOP!
That landing just does not get any easier!
The Wild West!
GENERAL STORE
BANK
SHERIFF
Holdup!
BANK
HELP! Big Bad Bob has just robbed the bank!
You cannot stop me now!

Follow me, Will!
To the horses!
Stop them! They have all the money for the new school!
SHERIFF
BAM!
Help is here!
BANK
It is Sheriff Dan! He will stop them.

Stop right there!
Wow! Now we will see some action!
Uh-oh.
I have an idea, Will. Follow me.
BANK
What in the . . .

These here barrels are magic, Bob!
I cannot get around them!
We will just go back that way, then!
Maybe he will catch them this time!
Or maybe he will not.
Oops.
I am dizzy.

Thank you kindly for tying up those barrels, Sheriff.
Now we can get away on our horses!
Time for action!
This way, Will!
Oh, no. Here we go again.
Got it!
Now!

AAAAAAAAHHHH!
Not so fast, Big Bad Bob!
SPLOOSH!
Now I have you! Sheriff Dan has saved the day again!
Hey . . .
The town is safe!
Sheriff Dan has saved the school!
Best rope in the West!
Way to go!

. . . *we* stopped them! Jill and Will!
Home again!
If I erase the code, it brings you back. You kids are lucky I was here.
Thanks, Grandpa Ben!
Sorry, Grandpa Ben.
One of these days, you kids will not be the only ones to have fun . . .
. . . I am certain of it!

Pirates!

Grandpa Ben is gone!
It looks like the code is right this time.
Well, where is Grandpa Ben?
I do not know why he would leave the slide open like this.
He might be in trouble. We have to go help him!
Sliding through time to save Grandpa!

SPLOOSH!
It is a good thing that Grandpa Ben can swim!
Well, so can we, but we cannot swim *up* a ship! How will we get up there?
Does that mean what I think it means?
Yep. Pirates.
SPLOOSH!
Saved by pirates! Cool!
"Cool" is not the word I was thinking of.

Some rescue!
Thank you!
Thank you? We do not say such things on a pirate ship, miss!
It is Red Nose the Pirate!
SWOOSH!
THUDD!
Well, what have we here?
Feed them to the fishes!
Hold on, Captain!

WHAT?
We could use some help cleaning the deck!
Well, now, that is a good point.
The ship is in sight! Ahoy!
All this time travel just to end up doing chores!
WE HAVE YOU NOW!
We have to stop this!
I thought we came to find Grandpa Ben.

Grandpa Ben can handle himself!
Sails away!
Yikes!
RIP!
Got you!
Do not worry, Captain! I will take care of these kids!
I have no time for this! I have a ship to catch!

Did you see that?
The pirates crash into the other ship!
BAM!
We are the only ones left!
Now we can save that ship!

Yes,
ve can!
Grandpa
Ben!
What are
you doing?
FIREWORKS
FIR
FIREWORKS
No time
to chat! Get up
that mast!
Not so fast, Red Nose!
CRASH!

We are saved!
WOW!
How will we get back? I thought you would erase the chalkboard!
I think this will work!
Home again!
We make a great team!
Well done, you two!
So . . . where to next time?